In the
Small, Small Pond

For David, still the one.

Imprints of Macmillan Publishing Group, LLC
175 Fifth Avenue
New York, NY 10010
mackids.com

Henry Holt® is a registered trademark of Henry Holt and Company, LLC. *Publishers since 1866.*
Square Fish and the Square Fish logo are trademarks of Macmillan and
are used by Henry Holt and Company under license from Macmillan.

Library of Congress Cataloging-in-Publication Data
Fleming, Denise.
In the small, small pond / Denise Fleming.
p.   cm.
Summary: Illustrations and rhyming text describe the activities of
animals living in and near a small pond as spring progresses to autumn.
[1. Pond animals—Ficiton. 2. Stories in rhyme.] I. Title.
PZ8.3.F6378 lm 1993   [E]—dc20   92-25770

Originally published in the United States by Henry Holt and Company
First Square Fish Edition: March 2013
Square Fish logo designed by Filomena Tuosto

ISBN 978-0-8050-2264-3 (Henry Holt hardcover)
42 41 40 39 38 37 36 35 34 33 32

ISBN 978-0-8050-5983-0 (Square Fish paperback)
40 39 38 37

AR: 2.0

In the
Small, Small Pond

Denise Fleming

Henry Holt and Company • New York

In the small, small

pond...

wiggle, jiggle,

tadpoles

wriggle

waddle, wade,

geese parade

hover,

shiver,

wings quiver

drowse,

doze,

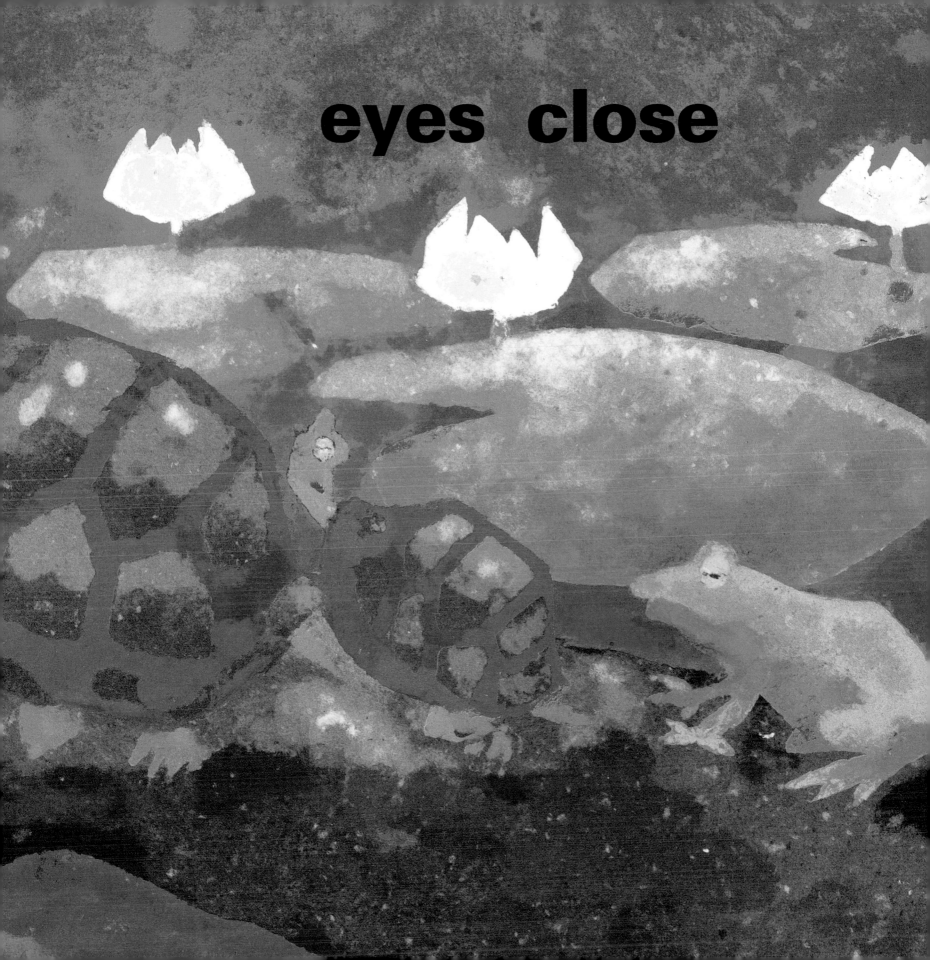

herons plunge

minnows scatter

circle, swirl,

whirligigs twirl

sweep, swoop,

swallows

swoop

click, clack,

claws crack

splish, splash, paws flash

pile,

pack,

muskrats
stack.

Chill breeze,

winter freeze...

cold night,

sleep tight,

small, small

pond.